TWINS vs. TRIPLETS

BACK-TO-SCHOOL BLITZ

Let the pranks begin! Read all the TWINS VS. TRIPLETS books!

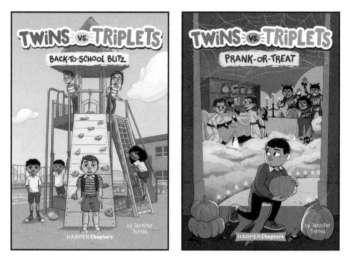

#1   #2

HARPER **Chapters**

TWiNS vs. TRiPLETS

BACK-TO-SCHOOL BLITZ

by Jennifer Torres

illustrated by Vanessa Flores

HARPER

An Imprint of HarperCollins*Publishers*

For James

Twins vs. Triplets #1: Back-to-School Blitz
Copyright © 2021 by HarperCollins Publishers
All rights reserved. Printed in the United States of America.
No part of this book may be used or reproduced in any manner
whatsoever without written permission except in the case of brief
quotations embodied in critical articles and reviews. For information
address HarperCollins Children's Books, a division of HarperCollins
Publishers, 195 Broadway, New York, NY 10007.
www.harperchapters.com

Library of Congress Control Number: 2020950475
ISBN 978-0-06-305945-0 — ISBN 978-0-06-305944-3 (paperback)

Typography by Torborg Davern
21 22 23 24 25   PC/LSCC   10 9 8 7 6 5 4 3 2 1
❖
First Edition

Table of Contents

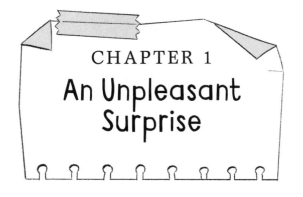

CHAPTER 1
An Unpleasant Surprise

PENCILS? Sharpened and tucked inside their pouch. Folders? Labeled and color coded. I checked and rechecked my list. Everything was in order, just the way I liked. I zipped my backpack shut.

"Gotta go, Mom," I called. "Can't be late on the first day of school!"

Mom was in the kitchen, blending her morning licuado, a mix of mango, banana, milk, ice, and just a little honey. Dad had already left for work.

"Wait just one momentito," she called back. "I want to see you off."

But I didn't want to wait, not even for a moment. I was ready to race out the front door. So ready that I had almost forgotten about the Romero twins. *Almost.*

I froze with my hand around the doorknob.

If I wasn't careful, I might crash through a wall of plastic wrap. Or step into a giant bowl of Jell-O. All thanks to Ash and Iris Romero. Also known as my awful next-door neighbors.

Mom walked over with her smoothie—and an umbrella. "Thought you might need this."

"Good idea!" It wasn't raining, but rain wasn't my problem. Last year, on the first day of second grade, the twins had rigged a jumbo-size jar of pickles to pour over my head as I stepped outside. My hair had smelled like vinegar for weeks.

"¿Estás listo?" Mom asked as I took the umbrella.

"Ready," I answered.

I opened the umbrella, then opened the door. Unfortunately, this year's unpleasant surprise came from below.

"Ack!" I jumped backward as red goop spilled out of a bucket and into the entryway.

Mom wrinkled her nose. "What is it?"

Cautiously, I dipped a finger into the ooze. It was stickier than my new school glue.

"Smells like . . . strawberry?"

Mom shrugged. "At least it's better than the pickles." She handed me her licuado and rolled up the rubber mat we had left in the entryway just in case. The floor underneath was sparkling clean.

"See? No hay problema," Mom said. "Don't worry, David. You can avoid those Travieso Twins just like you avoided this . . . whatever it is."

Traviesos, also known as troublemakers, was one of Mom's favorite nicknames for the twins. And they did everything they could to live up to it.

I had spent all summer ducking the shaving cream–filled balloons they tossed at me whenever I tried to cook in my homemade solar oven.

And scooping suds out of Mom's rose bushes after they filled our hose with dish soap.

And unwrapping my bike when they covered the whole thing, tires and all, in aluminum foil.

But life was about to get a whole lot

SPLAT!

easier. Mom and Dad had a meeting with the principal and worked things out so I would never have to be in the same class as Ash and Iris again. It was almost too good to believe: seven magnificent twin-free hours a day, five days a week. Starting now.

All I had to do was survive the walk to school. No hay problema.

¡Bien hecho! That means "well done!"

CHAPTER 2

Time to Go

MOM waved goodbye as I jogged down our front steps. Finally, I was on my way.

We had a tradition on Montecito Lane. All the kids on the block walked to school together on the first day. Emily Tran, from across the street, was already waiting on the sidewalk. Genevieve Sweeney stood next to her, carrying her ballet bag as usual. They were going into second grade.

I waved at Sonny Delgado when I saw him walking up the street. Last year, we were in the geography club together.

Sonny's little brother, Henry, clung to his arm. Henry was just starting kindergarten.

Ash and Iris were still in their front yard, posing for pictures. With their matching outfits and toothpaste-commercial smiles, they almost looked like the perfect angels most grown-ups seemed to think they were. *Almost.*

"Last one," Mrs. Romero chirped. "On the count of three, say, 'Best year ever!'"

"Best year ever," I whispered, too quietly for anyone else to hear.

Free from those Travieso Twins, it really would be. Mom's mom, my abuela, used to babysit Mrs. Romero back when she was a little girl. Mom said that meant our families were connected, and we should try to get along with the Romeros. But after four years with the twins as neighbors, we all agreed that just putting up with them was enough.

After at least a dozen more pictures, Ash and Iris joined us on the sidewalk with their rolling backpacks. "Well," Iris demanded, "what are we waiting for?"

Emily pointed toward the house on the other side of mine. "My mom says we have three new kids this year. Haven't you met them, David?"

My cheeks went hot as everyone looked at me. "Not yet." Last weekend, a moving truck had parked next door, where Mr. and Mrs. Charles used to live. I was really going to miss the Charleses. They always let me climb up their avocado tree when I needed a break from the twins.

Mom and Dad and I had watched as the movers carried box after box into the house.

"Looks like a family," Mom had said.

"Maybe there will be kids your age," Dad added, squeezing my shoulders.

They both sounded hopeful. But I wasn't so sure. After all, Ash and Iris were my age too. Look how well *that* had turned out.

Iris cleared her throat. *Ahem.* "It's time to go."

"Yeah," Ash said. He glanced at his watch. It was the kind that could send messages and even play music. "Says here it'll take us exactly eleven minutes and forty seconds to get to school. Definitely time to go."

Just then, a crash came from what used to be the Charleses' garage.

Emily shuddered. "Shouldn't we wait for the new kids? What if they don't know the way?"

Iris gritted her teeth. "I *said* it's time to go. And now we'll have to hurry."

Two chapters down! What do you think the Travieso Twins will get up to next?

CHAPTER 3

Better Keep Up

WE all knew better than to argue with Iris. Everyone stepped forward to line up behind her and Ash. Everyone except me, that is. I stepped back. I knew from experience that the best place to be was as far away from the twins as possible. If I was lucky, they would forget I was even there.

I unsnapped the front pocket of my backpack and pulled out my geography flash cards to review on the walk to school. I needed all the practice I could get if I wanted to be captain of our club, the Globetrotters.

But just as I was about to start studying the rivers of South America, Iris stopped. So suddenly that I almost crashed into Henry.

She turned to Ash. "How long did you say it would take to get to school?"

"Exactly eleven minutes and forty seconds."

Iris put a hand on her hip and tilted her head. "That's funny, because I'm pretty sure you said *eight* minutes."

Ash's forehead wrinkled. He looked as confused as I was.

Iris tilted her head even farther and stared hard at Ash. Then, slowly, he began to nod.

Uh-oh. The twins were doing that talking-without-talking thing again.

"*Now* I remember," Ash said. "And, actually, it was six minutes."

Then, with a flick of their wrists, the twins transformed their rolling backpacks into mini scooters and zipped away. The rest of us watched, stunned, until Iris yelled over her shoulder, "You better keep up if you don't want to wake up with a moldy old baloney sandwich on your pillow!"

Emily frowned. "Can they even do that?"

These were the twins. Anything was

possible. I jammed my flash cards back into my backpack. "I don't want to find out!"

We all scrambled to catch up.

We splashed through a puddle. We leaped over a pile of lawn clippings. We tore through a spiderweb. *Blegh!* Wispy threads stuck to my mouth.

Ahead of me, Sonny pulled Henry along by the wrist. Emily's braid came loose. Genevieve's ballet bag flew out behind her.

By the time we got to school, my shirt was half-untucked, and my socks were soaked from running through that puddle. No hay problema. I always traveled with an extra pair.

Ash and Iris, meanwhile, looked as perfectly put together as they always did. At the press of a button their scooters turned into backpacks again, the handlebars

lowering and the kickboards folding into hidden compartments.

Iris put both hands on her hips. "Next time," she said as we all caught our breath, "when I say it's time to go, that means it's time to go." She and Ash started to walk away. Then Iris stopped. "And tomorrow? We're going to get here in *five minutes*."

I hardly minded, though. I was starting third grade—*without* the Travieso Twins.

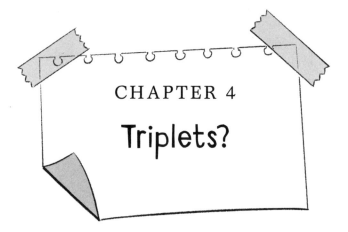

CHAPTER 4

Triplets?

I already knew my teacher, Mr. Kim. That's because he also coached the Globetrotters.

"David!" He held out his fist, and I bumped it with mine. "I hope you've been studying?"

"Only all summer."

"Don't forget, our first meeting is Thursday. For now, go ahead and find your seat."

Mr. Kim had taped name tags to every desk. Mine was in the second row—right behind Edith DeCastro's. This really was

the best year ever! Edith was my biggest competition for geography club captain. Luckily, she was also my best friend.

"Over here!" I waved as she walked through the door.

"Just the person I was looking for," she said. She sat and turned to face me. "Bet you don't know where the Great Plains are."

I cracked my knuckles. "Too easy. North Dakota, South Dakota, Montana, Nebras—"

"Nope."

"What do you mean, *nope?*"

A smile spread over Edith's face. "The great planes," she said, "are in the great airports. Get it? *Planes?*"

I rolled my eyes. I'd never admit it, but I had actually missed Edith's terrible geography puns.

The bell rang, and the classroom got quiet.

I should have known it wouldn't last.

Seconds later, the windows clattered as two boys and a girl smashed through the door all at once. They looked almost exactly alike, with round glasses and black hair.

Triplets?

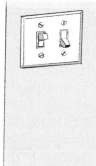

Principal Espinoza followed them in. "Mr. Kim, allow me to introduce our newest students, Bennie, Beckett, and Bird Benitez. They took a wrong turn on their way to class and found themselves . . . in the art closet."

For new kids, the triplets didn't seem a bit nervous. Not even about being late. The girl took off her glasses and wiped them on the edge of her shirt.

"I hope you'll be patient as I learn to tell you apart," Mr. Kim said. "Which one of you is—"

"Bennie?" The girl interrupted. "He is."

"She is," said the boys.

"Huh?" Mr. Kim looked down at his attendance sheet, then up at Principal Espinoza. She threw up her arms and walked away. "They're *all* yours."

Mr. Kim sighed. "On second thought, why don't you just take your seats."

Not until that moment did I notice the empty desks to the left and right of me. I gulped and turned around. That desk was empty too.

No es posible, I thought. But it was defi-nitely possible. The triplets sat down. I was surrounded.

"Now," Mr. Kim continued, "can I get a volunteer to help the Benitezes settle in?"

Edith's hand shot up. She was the kind of person who volunteered for everything.

Not me. I already had a bad feeling about these triplets. I sank lower in my seat and

tried to make myself invisible. But then something tickled my ear. I smacked at it and turned around.

"I'm Bird," the new girl whispered, waving a paintbrush.

"Did I see your hand, David?" Mr. Kim said. "Terrific. Please help our new friends get to know Arroyo Seco Elementary."

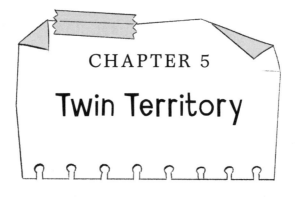

CHAPTER 5

Twin Territory

I'M normally not the kind of kid who says "recess" when someone asks what my favorite subject is. But that day, I was counting down the minutes until Mr. Kim said it was time to go outside. Between Bird poking me with her paintbrush, and Bennie and Beckett tossing notes over my head all morning, I needed a break. I'd give the triplets a tour of the playground, and then I'd be free to study in peace.

The Arroyo Seco playground was divided

into territories—just like a map. I pointed to the tetherball at the far end of the field. The fifth-grade zone. "They don't actually *play* tetherball," I explained. "They mostly just sit around, but the rest of us don't go over there."

Next was the sandbox. "It's mainly for the little kids."

Bird yawned. Bennie—or maybe it was Beckett—scratched his ear.

"There's the swing set, and over there are the handball courts. That's where I usually go. There's lots of shade, and it's almost always empty."

If the handball courts were a country, they'd be Malta. Very low risk of natural disasters. "Want to walk over?"

"Blegh!" Bird stuck her tongue out.

"Boring!" said Beckett or Bennie.

"Boring can be nice," I said. But they were still making those gagging faces. *"Fine.* How about the swings?" It was pretty safe as long as the twins didn't catch you swinging too high. They held the record for highest jump and wouldn't let anyone else even try to beat it.

"Nah," said Bird. "There." She pointed toward the one place I hadn't shown them. The one place I'd hoped they wouldn't notice.

In the middle of the playground was a tower attached to a spiral slide. There were four ways to the top: a pole, a rope ladder, a climbing wall, and some steps. All of it was Twin Territory.

"Trust me, you don't want to go up there," I said, trying to steer them away. The tower was like Iceland: volcanically active.

"Why not?" one of the boys asked.

"Yeah," said the other. "Why not?"

"It's just that . . . see, the twins . . ." I tried to explain. "We just don't want any trouble."

It was too late. Bird was halfway up the rope ladder. Her brothers were right behind her.

Already, a small crowd was gathering at the base.

"Whoa, David, I can't believe you're going up," Sonny said.

"*Me?* No! I'm not—"

Then someone cleared their throat behind

me. *Ahem.*

Once again, I tried to make myself invisible.

Once again, it didn't work.

"David Suárez." I turned around. Iris's hands were on her hips. "Please explain why you let the new kids climb *our* tower."

CHAPTER 6
Señor Stripes

"I didn't!" I said. "I tried to stop them!"

"That's not what I saw." Ash tapped his watch. A tiny picture popped up: me and the triplets, looking up at the tower.

"But—"

Iris held up her hand. "Just get them down."

"And there won't be any trouble," Ash added.

"What kind of trouble?" It was Bird. Her legs dangled over the edge of the tower.

"How about tetherball?" I called up. I would rather get chased away by fifth graders than find out what kind of trouble the twins had in mind.

"No thanks," Bird said. "I know a better game. It's rainbow tag, and you're all it!"

As soon as she said it, Bennie and Beckett took off their shoes and dumped them out over the railing.

Something powdery, like rainbow-colored snow, fluttered onto our heads.

I caught some in my hand and rubbed it between my fingers. "It's ground-up chalk! From the art closet!"

Ash sneezed. Iris huffed. Her shirt was covered in chalk dust. "This outfit was *brand new*! Ash, what color is it?"

AH-CHOO!

Ash squinted. "Sort of pinkish, yellowish—"

"Not the chalk," she said. "The *other thing*."

"Oh, the *other thing*." Ash tapped his watch again. "Purple and orange."

"Nobody move!" Iris yelled as they bolted back toward the classrooms.

Nobody dared.

"Do you think they went to get a teacher?" someone asked.

I didn't think so. Tattling wasn't the twins' style.

Sure enough, when they returned, it wasn't with a teacher. It was with a backpack.

"Hey, that's mine!" Bird shouted.

I knew you should never underesti-
mate the Travieso Twins. Still, even I was
impressed. "How did you know?"

 Ash showed me the
picture on his watch:
moving boxes on the
Benitezes' porch. Right
on top was Bird's
purple-and-orange
backpack. "You didn't
think you were the only
one spying on the new neighbors,
did you?"

Before I could argue, I saw Iris pull out
Bird's lunch bag. She peeked inside and
took out a cookie. "Chocolate chip, my
favorite!" She took an enormous bite.

Bird just shrugged, reached into her sock,
and pulled out another cookie. "I always
carry extra."

Then Iris rummaged deeper inside the backpack. Finally, she pulled out a stuffed tiger. It was missing an eye and its fur was all frazzled. "What's this? Does Birdie Benitez still sleep with a stuffie?"

"You leave Señor Stripes alone!" Bird yelled.

She slid down the slide. One of the brothers scrambled down the ladder. The other scurried down the steps. They charged at Iris.

Iris didn't move until, at the last second, she threw the tiger—at me. "Run!"

I ran. What else could I do? After so many years of running from the twins, I had a lot of practice.

As the triplets chased me around the playground, Ash and Iris climbed to the top of the tower. *Their* tower.

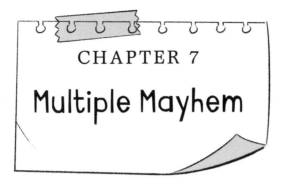

CHAPTER 7

Multiple Mayhem

"FLASH cards?" I asked Edith as we walked out to recess the next day. Rival or not, she was the best study partner.

"Sure," she said, raising an eyebrow. "I can help you."

"You mean, I can help *you*." I raised an eyebrow back at her but couldn't help smiling as we found a shady place to sit.

Before we started, I scanned the playground. Everything *seemed* calm. But you couldn't get too comfortable with twins—and now triplets—around.

I spotted the twins right away. They were on top of the tower. Iris scowled down while Ash seemed to be inspecting the ceiling. Strange, but not too worrisome.

What *did* worry me was the triplets. "What are they up to?" I muttered.

"There." Edith pointed at the sandbox where Bennie, Beckett, and Bird sat quietly with their water bottles. "¿No hay problema?"

I exhaled. "No hay problema. Let's start with state capitals."

But we only made it from Albany through Phoenix before a roar rose from the sandbox.

"¡A la carga!" Bird hollered, clutching Señor Stripes in her raised fist.

Edith and I watched, mouths wide open, as the triplets ran toward the tower. A pack of screaming kindergartners raced after them, carrying buckets of mud. They dumped it on the slide, poured it on the steps, drizzled it over the rope ladder, smeared it on the pole, and splashed it on the climbing wall.

Iris paced at the top, her cheeks blazing. "Stop that!"

The kindergartners didn't stop, though. Maybe no one had told them the twins ruled the playground. When their buckets were empty, they just ran back to the sandbox for more mud.

Ash darted from the slide, to the steps, to the ladder, to the pole, to the wall, looking for a way down.

"What's the matter?" Bird teased. "Stuck?"
Iris lifted her chin. "We are *not* stuck."

But everyone could see the twins were trapped. At the end of recess they had no choice but to slosh down the swampy slide. When they got to the bottom, their perfect white sneakers were covered in mud.

I knew the twins would get even. I just didn't know how. I didn't have to wait long to find out.

On Wednesday, Ash and Iris beat the triplets to the tower, but only stayed on top a minute before sliding down again.

Sospechoso, I thought. Suspicious. Even more suspicious was what Iris did next.

"Oh no! We left our delicious chocolate chip cookies up there," she announced, a little too loudly. "David Suárez, guard the tower until we get back."

"But—" I protested. I wanted to study with Edith, not get dragged into more multiple mayhem.

"I said *guard it*!" Iris snapped.

As soon as she and Ash were out of sight, Bird's head popped out from behind the handball court. "¡Vámonos!" Let's go!

Uh-oh. I raced to the tower, but it was no use. When I tried to block Bird from the ladder, Bennie—or maybe it was Beckett—sprang up the steps. When I tried to block Beckett—or maybe it was Bennie—from the steps, Bird scurried up the pole.

My stomach turned a somersault when all three of them made it up and Bird yelled, "Get the cookies!"

I squeezed my eyes shut. I couldn't watch. The twins would be furious.

Then one of the Benitez boys said, "These taste funny."

"Spicy," Bird agreed

"Gah!" yelled the other brother. "My mouth is on fire!"

A moment later, they slid down the pole, one after another. Sweat dripped down their faces. "Water!" Bird shouted.

"What happened to *them*?" Edith said, staring.

I should've guessed sooner. "Habanero chocolate chip. It's a Romero specialty." Ash and Iris had baked a batch for my birthday last year.

The twins strolled back to the playground as the Benitez brothers shoved their way toward the drinking fountain.

"So, Birdie," Iris said, "how did you like the cookies?"

Bird glared back, her eyes watering.

"Deliciosas," she said finally.

CHAPTER 8
Back-to-School Blitz

BY Thursday, I didn't know what to expect. The triplets were quiet all morning. Too quiet.

Then, during math, Bird pinched the back of my neck. Hard.

"Ow!"

Mr. Kim glanced up. "David? Something wrong?"

Before I could answer, Bird jumped out of her seat. "It was a hornet, Mr. Kim! It stung David!"

Elle Maguire screamed. "Where?"

"Right behind you!" said Beckett, or at least I thought it was him.

"And over there!" Bennie (I think) hollered. "Another one!"

"Get it away from me!" said Ricky Chavez.

"Please," Mr. Kim said, "let's stay calm."

Too late. Everyone was out of their seats, shooing an imaginary swarm of hornets.

"Thanks," Bird whispered in my ear.

53

Then, with the whole class distracted, the triplets snuck away.

I could guess where to.

Sure enough, they were waiting on top of the tower when recess started. They had piled up the dodgeballs and hurled them at anyone who came too close.

We all steered clear until Iris yelled, "Don't just stand there! Throw them back!"

Before long, the playground was like one giant dodgeball game. Kindergartners

pelted second graders. Fourth graders took aim at first graders.

I hated dodgeball. I covered my head with my arms and tried to make it to the sandbox without getting hit. As I crept away, I overheard Iris hiss, "Now's our chance." I watched as Ash darted behind the bushes and brought back a bag full of water balloons, the same kind he and Iris had thrown at me all summer. Only these weren't filled with water. Or even shaving cream.

One of them smacked the tower. Red ooze splattered over everyone underneath.

"It's in my hair!" Emily said. "Disgusting! And sticky!"

Another balloon exploded against the slide. *Whap!* And then another.

"What is this stuff?" Sonny said.

The triplets ducked behind the railing just as a balloon hit it. The dodgeballs stopped flying, but I knew this wasn't over.

"What's the matter?" Iris called up. "Stuck?"

The triplets didn't answer.

That's when I realized Ash was missing. He was almost always right beside his sister. Where had he gone? More important, what was he doing?

A moment later, I knew the answers to both questions. Ash dove *under* the tower. He grabbed a cord. The same kind of cord I had found on my porch after last year's pickle prank.

"Edith, Sonny, look out!" I ran back to warn them.

But I wasn't fast enough.

Iris shouted, "Now!"

Ash yanked the cord. A bucket hanging from the roof of the tower toppled. Red goop gushed over everyone underneath.

"AUGH!" we all yelled as gluey red goo splattered over our heads and faces.

Still, the triplets were silent.

"You'll have to come down sooner or later," Ash said.

We watched, frozen, until we finally heard Bird's voice call, "All right, we're coming down."

Then Bennie, Bird, and Beckett stood. All three were neat and dry under an open umbrella.

"*What?!*" Iris screeched. She turned to me. "You warned them, didn't you, David Suárez?"

But before she could say anything else, the triplets rolled down the slide—on the twins' backpack scooters!

That's when Ms. MacMillan, the recess assistant, finally blew her whistle. That whole time, she had been helping a first grader with a bloody nose.

"No scooters on the—"

Ms. MacMillan stopped when she noticed the strawberry sludge. Her eyes followed the cord from the top of the tower down to the bottom— where Ash was still holding it.

"Ash and Iris, I'm surprised at you!"

"But, Ms. MacMillan," Iris said, smiling sweetly, "we weren't . . . I mean, we didn't . . ."

Ms. MacMillan didn't let her finish.

"You'll stay after school to clean this mess," Ms. MacMillan said. "And you'll spend the rest of recess on the bench."

Iris shot me an icy glare as they left the playground.

"As for the rest of you," Ms. MacMillan went on, "things have gotten out of hand."

I agreed.

"We need some order out here."

Exactly.

"We need a safety monitor."

Ugh. Not even Edith would volunteer for that.

"David Suárez, I know I can count on you to make sure everyone plays by the rules. Otherwise, I'm afraid the playground will be off-limits."

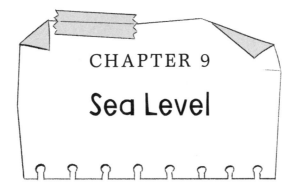

CHAPTER 9

Sea Level

¡QUÉ desastre! What a disaster! Being safety monitor was even worse than getting soaked in pickle juice. No one could guess what the twins and triplets would do next, but somehow I was supposed to stop it. And if I didn't, it would be my fault we lost the playground.

My shoulders didn't relax until the bell rang at the end of the day. At last it was time for geography club. The one place I didn't have to worry about misbehaving multiples.

63

Mr. Kim asked Edith and me to arrange the desks in a circle while he ran to the teachers' lounge to get the snacks.

"So," Edith said, trying to sound casual. "Think you're gonna be captain this year?"

I tried to sound casual too, but it was hard to contain my excitement. "Maybe." I shrugged. The truth was I couldn't wait to show Mr. Kim I was the right person to lead the Globetrotters to victory.

The rest of the club arrived, and Mr. Kim

returned with juice boxes and pretzels. We passed them around as the meeting began.

"Since this is our first meeting of the year," Mr. Kim said, "I thought we'd start with one of the easier topics: US geography."

I sat up straighter. US geography was my strongest area.

Mr. Kim went around the circle, asking questions as we all crunched pretzels. He started with Edith.

"Which state is home to Mount Hood, a volcanic peak that last erupted in 1865?"

I made a mental list of states with active volcanoes. But before I could get past Hawaii and Alaska, I started wondering, *Are the twins about to erupt too?*

I almost didn't notice when Edith answered, "Oregon."

"Correct!" Mr. Kim said and rang a bell.

Next was Cora Van Buskirk.

"Which state's climate is better for growing sugar beets, Florida or Minnesota?"

I sure hope the triplets never get their hands on any sugar beets. I'd hate to be in a dodgeball game with those.

"Minnesota!" Cora answered.

By the time Mr. Kim got to me, my palms had started to sweat. I couldn't seem to focus.

"Which is the oldest capital city in the United States?"

What a relief! Edith and I had studied the state capitals. I knew them backward and forward.

Only, suddenly, I didn't. "Umm . . . Boston?"

Edith gasped.

"Close," Mr. Kim said. "Boston is the second oldest. The oldest is Santa Fe, New Mexico."

Every round was the same. It was as if the twins and triplets had taken over my whole brain and there was no room left for geography.

After the meeting ended, Edith nudged me. "Hey," she said. "What do you and Death Valley have in common?"

"I don't know," I mumbled. "What?"

"You're both below C-level. Get it? Like *sea* level?"

"Ha." Edith's puns weren't so funny anymore.

68

"C'mon, I was only kidding," she said. "You know I wouldn't study half as hard if I didn't have you to compete with."

That made me feel a little better, but not much.

How do you think David will solve this problem?

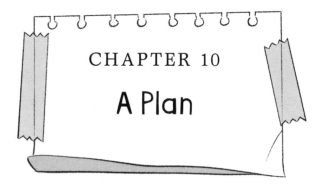

CHAPTER 10

A Plan

I couldn't eat that night. Arroz con pollo was my favorite dinner, but I just pushed the rice and chicken around my plate.

"¿Qué pasa?" Dad asked.

"What's wrong?" I replied. "Only *everything*."

I told Mom and Dad how the best year ever was turning out to be the worst. How triplet trouble was almost as bad as twin torture.

Just as I finished, an avocado sailed over our backyard. The Benitezes had been launching them at the Romeros all evening. "See?"

Mom patted my arm, then got up to bring us a plate of chocolate quesadillas, a dessert we made up when I was younger. They're like regular quesadillas, only instead of cheese inside, there's chocolate. I wasn't sure they were going to help. But I didn't think they would hurt either.

"Well, mijo, you can tell Ms. MacMillan you don't want the job," she said. "But maybe you can turn this problem into an opportunity."

I thought about that as I dried the dishes later, and I remembered what Edith had said about competition. By bedtime, I had an idea.

I couldn't stop the twins and triplets from competing over the tower. But maybe I could change *how*—and save recess in the process.

I told Edith my plan first thing Friday.

"I guess this means you need my help again?" she asked, raising an eyebrow.

"Definitely."

We watched the clock tick toward recess. With five minutes to spare, I raised my hand.

"David?"

"Can I leave early?" I asked, my heart

thumping. "It's a . . . safety monitor thing."

Mr. Kim hesitated. "Ms. MacMillan didn't say—"

"It's true!" Edith interrupted. "He has to leave. We both do."

"Well," Mr. Kim said, "I suppose—"

"Thank you!"

We sprang from our seats and sprinted to the tower. So far, so good.

CHAPTER 11

Lightning Round

"DAVID Suárez," Iris growled when recess started, "you better come down before I climb up."

Bird was right behind her. "You mean, before *I* climb up."

"Hold on," I yelled back. "I think I can settle this."

"How?" said Bennie, or possibly Beckett.

"A showdown," I said. "A *geography* showdown."

Bird scrunched her nose. "A *what?*"

I explained the rules. There were fifteen

steps and fifteen rungs leading to the top of the tower. If a Romero answered a question correctly, the twins would move up a step. If a Benitez answered correctly, the triplets would climb a rung.

"First one to the top wins *everything.*"

"This is ridiculous," Iris said.

Edith leaned over the railing. "Afraid you don't know the answers?"

"No."

"Prove it," said Bird. Beckett and Bennie folded their arms over their chests.

"*Fine,*" Iris said.

It was working! "Maybe you should shake on it." I said. "First team to the top wins the tower."

Bird spit into her palm and held out her hand to Iris.

"Gross!" Iris scowled. "We agree, okay?"

"Did everyone hear that?" I called.

The whole playground, even the fifth graders, cheered.

"It's a deal." I pulled out my flash cards. "First question goes to the twins: Which mountain range is longer, the Rockies or the Sierra Nevada? And no using your watch!"

Iris cupped her hands and whispered in Ash's ear. He shook his head, then whispered back. Finally, Iris answered, "The Rockies."

"Correct."

They climbed one step.

"Next question: In what order do the directions appear on a compass?"

"North, South, East, West!" Bird blurted.

The triplets started climbing.

"Wait! I'm sorry, but that's incorrect. The answer is North, East, South, West. *Never Eat Soggy Waffles.*"

The triplets grumbled, but they got off the ladder.

Everything was going according to plan.

That is, until the bell rang with the twins and triplets tied, fifteen to fifteen.

No winner. ¡Qué desastre!

"Now what?" Bird said.

"What a waste of time," complained Iris.

The crowd began to rumble.

"This stinks!" someone shouted.

I shuffled my flash cards, trying to think what to do.

Then Edith stuck two fingers in her mouth and whistled.

"You're forgetting about the lightning round," she said.

We had never discussed this. "The lightning round?"

"That's right," she said. "Whoever answers this next question correctly wins. Agreed?"

"Agreed!" they all shouted.

Edith looked at me, and I nodded. Even though I still didn't know exactly what was happening.

"Okay," she said. "The final question is: Where are the Great Plains?"

Ms. MacMillan blew her whistle. We were all going to get in trouble if we didn't hurry back to class. Why would Edith pick such a difficult question? There were ten states to remember.

The twins and triplets started shouting names, none of them correct. The crowd began to boo.

Edith nudged me in the ribs. "I repeat, *whoever* answers correctly wins."

"Oh!" I finally understood.

I leaned over the railing. I cleared my throat. "The answer is Montana, North Dakota, South Dakota, Wyoming, Nebraska, Kansas, Colorado, Oklahoma, Texas, and New Mexico."

Then I turned back to Edith. "And the great airports."

"Correct!"

I didn't even need a flash card.

CHAPTER 12

Best Year Ever

RECESS was a whole lot easier after the geography showdown.

As winner, I decided the top of the tower would be open to anyone who needed a quiet place to sit. And anyone passing through on their way to the slide, of course.

The twins didn't give up trying to rule the playground. But without their perch on the tower, they couldn't shout down orders anymore.

The triplets didn't stop looking for trouble. But at least they weren't picking fights with the twins. I did have a bad feeling about that pit they were digging in the sandbox, though.

I finally had some peace. Just in time too. I needed to study so I could show Mr. Kim I had what it took to be captain, despite my terrible performance the week before.

At our next club meeting, the subject was world deserts. I got every question right.

"Bet you don't know this one," Edith said. "What makes the Sonoran Desert so smart?" She paused. "It has so many degrees! Get it?"

We all groaned.

"Thank you, Edith," Mr. Kim said. "Now, I have a special announcement to make, one I know you've been waiting for."

We all leaned forward. My heart raced.

"This year," Mr. Kim went on, "the Globetrotters will have two captains. Edith DeCastro and David Suárez, congratulations!"

Edith and I looked at each other. "Best year ever!" we said at the same time. But before we had a chance to celebrate, there was a thud and a clatter at the door.

Beckett, Bird, and Bennie had just squeezed through the door.

"We're here to sign up," said Bird.

There had to be some mistake. "This is geography club," I explained.

"We know," Bird said. Bennie and Beckett grabbed the last juice boxes. "We had fun answering all those weird questions, so we decided to join."

That definitely wasn't part of the plan.

Ahem.

Oh no.

"Move over," Iris said.

"Yeah," said Ash. "We're joining too."

"But . . . but," I sputtered. *"Why?"*

Iris sat at an empty desk. "You didn't think we'd just let you win, did you?"

¡Qué desastre!

FUN AND GAMES

THINK

Draw a map of your school playground or park from memory. If you were asked to show a new student around, what would you say about each area? What's your favorite spot to hang out?

FEEL

In the book, David is excited about the first day of school . . . until he meets the triplets. Write down all the words that pop into your head when you think about school. Then circle all the words that make you feel more excited about day one!

ACT

Want to know how David's mom makes chocolate quesadillas?

1. Lightly butter one side of a flour tortilla.

2. Place the tortilla butter side down in a pan on the stove top.

3. Sprinkle 2 tbsp. of chocolate chips and a little cinnamon on top.

4. With an adult's help, heat the tortilla until the chocolate melts.

5. Fold the tortilla in half like a sandwich.

6. ¡Buen provecho! Enjoy!

Jennifer Torres is an award-winning author of books for young readers. She loves writing stories about home, friendship, and unexpected courage inspired by her Mexican American heritage. Jennifer lives with her husband and two daughters in Southern California. She loves it there . . . even though it has its *faults*. (Get it? Like earthquake faults?)

Vanessa Flores is an illustrator and writer raised on plátanos and old-school salsa. She was once trapped in her own bedroom because her sister had covered the doorknob in petroleum jelly. She is proud to be part of a diverse group of artists and Latinx people in her community in Orlando, Florida.